D1473762

HEPHAESTUS

GOD OF FIRE, METALWORK, AND BUILDING

BY TERI TEMPLE   ILLUSTRATED BY ROBERT SQUIER

Published by The Child's World®
1980 Lookout Drive • Mankato, MN 56003-1705
800-599-READ • www.childsworld.com

ISBN 9781503832572
LCCN 2018957714

Printed in the United States of America

About the Author
Teri Temple is a former elementary school teacher who
now travels the country as an event coordinator. She
developed a love for mythology as a fifth-grade student
following a unit in class on Greek and Roman history. Teri
likes to spend her free time hanging out with her family,
biking, hiking, and reading. She lives in Minnesota with
her husband and their golden retriever, Buddy.

About the Illustrator
Robert Squier has illustrated dozens of books for children.
He enjoys drawing almost anything, but he really loves
drawing dinosaurs and mythological beasts. Robert Squier
lives in New Hampshire with his wife, son, and a puggle
named Q.

CONTENTS

INTRODUCTION

Long ago in ancient Greece and Rome, most people believed that gods and goddesses ruled their world. Storytellers shared the adventures of these gods to help explain all the mysteries of life. The gods were immortal, meaning they lived forever. Their stories were full of love and tragedy, fearsome monsters, brave heroes, and struggles for power. The storytellers wove aspects of Greek customs and beliefs into the tales. Some stories told of the creation of the world and the origins of the gods. Others helped explain natural events such as earthquakes and storms. People believed the tales, which over time became myths.

The ancient Greeks and Romans worshiped the gods by building temples and statues in their honor. They felt the gods would protect and guide them. People passed down the myths through the generations by word of mouth. Later, famous poets such as Homer and Hesiod wrote them down. Today, these myths give us a unique look at what life was like in ancient Greece more than 2,000 years ago.

ANCIENT GREEK SOCIETIES

In ancient Greece, cities, towns, and their surrounding farmlands were called city-states. These city-states each had their own governments. They made their own laws. The individual city-states were very independent. They never joined to become one whole nation. They did, however, share a common language, religion, and culture.

MOUNT OLYMPUS
The mountaintop home
of the 12 Olympic gods

Aegean Sea

*Mediterranean
Sea*

Sea of Crete

ANCIENT
GREECE

CRETE

CHARACTERS
AND PLACES

APHRODITE *(af-roh-DY-tee)*
Goddess of love and beauty; born of the sea foam; wife of Hephaestus; mother of Eros

ARES *(AIR-eez)*
God of war; son of Zeus and Hera; possible father of Eros

ATHENA *(a-THEE-na)*
Goddess of wisdom; daughter of Zeus

CYCLOPES *(SY-klohps)*
One-eyed giants; children of Gaea and Uranus

HARMONIA *(hahr-MOH-nee-uh)*
Daughter of Ares and Aphrodite; wife of Cadmus

HERA *(HEER-uh)*
Queen of the gods; married to Zeus

MOMUS *(MOH-muhs)*
God of ridicule; judged a contest of the gods

PANDORA *(pan-DOR-uh)*
First woman on Earth; created by Hephaestus; opened the box of evils out of curiosity

THETIS *(THEE-tus)*
Daughter of a sea nymph; mother of Greek hero Achilles; helped raise Hephaestus

ZEUS *(ZOOS)* Supreme ruler of the heavens and weather and of the gods who lived on Mount Olympus; youngest son of Cronus and Rhea; married to Hera; father of many gods and heroes

HEPHAESTUS *(huh-FES-tuhs)*
God of fire, metalwork, and building; son of Zeus and Hera; married to Aphrodite

MOUNT ETNA
An active volcano in Sicily; underneath it was the workshop of Hephaestus

OLYMPIAN GODS
Demeter, Hermes, Hephaestus, Aphrodite, Ares, Hera, Zeus, Poseidon, Athena, Apollo, Artemis, and Dionysus

TROJAN WAR
War between the ancient Greeks and Trojans

TITANS *(TIE-tinz)*
The 12 children of Gaea and Cronus; godlike giants that are said to represent the forces of nature

THE GOD OF FIRE, METALWORK, AND BUILDING

Hephaestus was the mighty god of fire. He was also the best blacksmith and craftsman in the universe. Yet Hephaestus did not have a noble start in life. There are two versions of how Hephaestus came into the world. Hephaestus was the second son of Zeus and Hera, the king and queen of the Olympic gods. Ares, the god of war, was their first son. Hephaestus was as gentle as his brother Ares was cruel. The brothers lived with their parents high atop Mount Olympus. Zeus and Hera ruled the universe with their siblings Poseidon, Hades, Demeter, and Hestia.

In one version of Hephaestus's story, he was born as a perfect god, just like all the other gods. One day he tried to protect his mother from being punished by Zeus. This made Zeus furious. So Zeus took Hephaestus by the foot and hurled him from the heavens. Hephaestus fell all the way to Earth. His landing was abrupt and violent. It left Hephaestus disabled. Hephaestus returned to Mount Olympus humbled and unable to walk well. There the other gods laughed behind his back. It was a rocky start for the god of fire.

The second version of Hephaestus's story is not much happier. Hera was angry with Zeus for having his daughter Athena, who sprang from his forehead. So she decided to have a child all on her own. Hera became pregnant by the sheer force of her will. When her son Hephaestus was born, Hera's joy turned to disgust. Hephaestus had been born with a clubbed foot and would be lame. A lame person has difficulty walking because of an injury to the foot or leg. Hephaestus was also ugly. Hera threw him right off Mount Olympus.

Hephaestus fell for nine days and nights before landing in the ocean. Two sea nymphs found him near the island of Lemnos. The sea nymphs, Thetis and Eurynome, rescued Hephaestus. They took him to their underwater cave. Together they raised him for the first nine years of his life. Hephaestus began to learn his craft in the secret cave. He collected pearls and jewels from the ocean floor. Then Hephaestus made them into beautiful pieces of jewelry.

THETIS AND ACHILLES

Thetis helped raise Hephaestus, but she also had a son named Achilles. She wanted to make Achilles immortal like the gods. Thetis knew the river Styx in the underworld had magical properties. So Thetis held Achilles by the heel and dipped him in the river. The parts of his body that touched the river became very strong. Achilles had just one weak spot—the heel where his mother held him. It would be his undoing. Achilles was killed during the Trojan War when an arrow pierced his heel. Today the expression "Achilles' heel" refers to a person's weakness.

Hephaestus grew up to be the god of fire, craftsmen, and metal-workers. He was very fond of artists and sculptors. Hephaestus was also the black-smith of the gods. In ancient Greece many blacksmiths were lame. This disability made it so they could no longer work as warriors, hunters, or farmers. Hephaestus became the god with a special interest in helping the lame.

The other gods admired Hephaestus for his skills as a craftsman. As the only working god, Hephaestus was strong and full of life. His work at the blacksmith's forge gave him a thick neck and heavily muscled arms. Hephaestus was often shown as a fully bearded middle-aged man. Hephaestus was hairy and constantly sweaty, which did not add to his charm. Despite his ugly appearance, Hephaestus was a gentle and peace-loving god. He was the opposite of his fiery brother, Ares. These two siblings would become rivals.

HEPHAESTUS'S DISABILITY

While other gods were shown as physically perfect, Hephaestus was not. The god of fire was always portrayed with his disability. The ancient Greeks may have made Hephaestus this way because of what really happened to blacksmiths in ancient times. Blacksmiths were often poisoned by their work. Blacksmiths added arsenic to the bronze they used. Arsenic is a poison. Arsenic poisoning often results in lameness. Hephaestus did not let his disability slow him down. He is often credited with inventing the first wheelchair.

One of Hephaestus's first jobs was to build the palace for the gods on Mount Olympus. He used gold and metals of every color to create beautiful designs all over the palace. He is considered by many to be the father of invention. Hephaestus first had to create the tools he needed. He made hammers, tongs, and anvils. Hephaestus even built robots of gold and silver to help him in his workshop.

Hephaestus was not just talented. He was generous as well. He created thrones, beautiful jewelry, chariots, and strong weapons for his fellow Olympic gods. For

ANCIENT GREEK CRAFTSMEN

Shops in ancient Greece were often small and family run. Family members worked with a few slaves. What the individual craftsmen made depended on the size of the city-state they lived in. In the smaller towns, a blacksmith might make swords, plows, axes, and other tools. In a larger city, he would specialize in making just one product.

Hermes he made winged sandals and a messenger hat. Zeus requested a breastplate from Hephaestus, called the Aegis. Hephaestus even fastened the head of the Gorgon Medusa to it to make it more powerful. One look at the snake-haired Gorgon could turn a person to stone. For Achilles and Heracles, Hephaestus made armor and weapons. Hephaestus also created the silver arrows of Apollo and Artemis. He even gave Eros his bow and arrows of love. If it was magical or finely made metalwork, Hephaestus was credited with making it in the ancient myths.

Ancient Greeks believed Hephaestus was also the god of volcanoes. His workshops were said to be located under volcanoes. Helping Hephaestus in his workshops were the mighty Cyclopes. The Cyclopes were the one-eyed giant sons of Gaea, or Mother Earth. The giants were also great blacksmiths. They had helped Zeus defeat the Titans during the war to control the universe. The Cyclopes created Poseidon's trident, Hades's helmet of invisibility, and Zeus's thunderbolts. The Cyclopes stayed on after the war to help Hephaestus build weapons for the gods. The sounds of their hammers could be heard all over Greece. The Cyclopes towered over humans and had amazing strength. This made them good assistants to Hephaestus. Running a blacksmith's forge was hard work.

Volcanoes

Ancient Greeks did not understand how volcanoes worked. One legend said volcanoes came from Typhon, a hideous 100-headed monster that spewed lava and fiery rocks from its mouths. In the story, Zeus stuck the monster Typhon under Mount Etna to stop its mischief. Mount Etna is one of the world's tallest active volcanoes. It is located on the island of Sicily. The ancient people believed Typhon was responsible for all volcanic eruptions on Earth. Hephaestus's workshop was also in Mount Etna. There he hammered molten ore.

The god Apollo later killed the Cyclopes and their sons. He wanted revenge for his son Asclepius's murder. Zeus committed the murder with his thunderbolts, but Apollo could not go after Zeus. Instead he killed the makers of the thunderbolts.

Hephaestus had three sisters. One was Hebe, the lovely goddess of youth. Eileithyia was another. She was the gentle goddess of childbirth. Then there was Athena. She came into the world with a battle cry. In one version of Hephaestus's birth, he was there before Athena was born. It began when Zeus swallowed Metis, the first of his many wives and loves. Zeus had heard that their unborn

child would one day overthrow him. He swallowed his wife to get rid of the threat. Zeus soon began having pounding headaches. When Zeus could stand it no more, he cried for help. Hephaestus ran and got his axe. In one blow he split open his father's forehead. Out jumped Athena as a full-grown warrior.

Hephaestus could not help but like Athena. He just could not figure out how to win her favor. Since both were gods of craftsmen, they shared a common interest. The two gods spent hours in Hephaestus's workshop perfecting their skills. Hephaestus even taught Athena how to work the forge. This was the furnace he used to heat up metal. When Hephaestus let Athena know of his love for her, she rejected him. He was heartbroken. Hephaestus decided that he would win the hand of one even more beautiful than Athena. He set his sights on Aphrodite.

LIBRA CONSTELLATION

The Libra constellation is located in the southern sky. It is the seventh sign of the zodiac. The ancient Greeks believed it represented weighing scales. The scales were those of the goddess of justice, Astraea. She was a daughter of Zeus. When Astraea left Earth, Zeus placed her in the sky as the constellation Virgo. He then placed Astraea's scales beside her. Ancient Greeks believed that Hephaestus created the scales and was their protector.

Hephaestus soon saw his next opportunity. Like all of the gods on Mount Olympus, he admired the goddess Aphrodite. It was hard not to respond to her charms. Aphrodite was, after all, the goddess of love and beauty. Hephaestus was sure she would never notice him. He felt she could never love someone as ugly as him. His luck was soon to change, however.

Hephaestus never forgot the cruel treatment he received from his mother, Hera. As a master craftsman, he used his skills to create a beautiful golden throne.

Hephaestus gave it to Hera as a gift. Unable to resist, Hera accepted the magnificent throne. But as soon as Hera sat on the throne, she was trapped. None of the other gods could figure out how to release her. When they asked Hephaestus to free Hera, he refused. Then Dionysus, the god of wine, got Hephaestus drunk. And Hephaestus finally agreed to free Hera. Hephaestus drove a hard bargain, though. He would only do so if Hera promised him Aphrodite as his wife. The deal was sealed and the two were married.

Hephaestus wanted to make his wife happy. He used his skill to create a girdle for her. A girdle is a piece of women's clothing that is worn around the waist and chest. It was made of the finest gold. Hephaestus wove magic into the girdle's design. It was to be his greatest gift. But the girdle's magic worked too well. The girdle made all men fall hopelessly in love with its wearer. Combined with Aphrodite's beauty, no one could resist its power. Aphrodite loved her gift and used it to trap all sorts of gods and men, including Hephaestus's brother Ares.

Aphrodite did not like the lame and ugly Hephaestus. She much preferred his more handsome brother Ares. So Aphrodite and Ares began to meet in secret. They were sure they could keep Hephaestus in the dark about their affair. But secrets did not last long on Mount Olympus. Soon Hephaestus found out. Sad and angry, he set a trap for them. Hephaestus created a magical net. It was made of nearly invisible bronze links.

HARMONIA'S NECKLACE

Hephaestus was not always kind in his gift giving. Hephaestus held a grudge against Ares and Aphrodite for betraying him. Hephaestus was still angry over their affair. So Hephaestus gave their daughter Harmonia a cursed necklace as a wedding gift. The necklace would only bring death and misfortune to those who possessed it. It doomed Harmonia and her offspring to endless tragedy.

One night as Ares and Aphrodite slept, Hephaestus cast his net over them. Hephaestus then brought all the gods to judge the trapped pair. He hoped the embarrassment would cause Ares to end the affair.

In the end, the other gods could not blame Ares. After all, who could resist Aphrodite? Hephaestus went on to have other loves and many children, but none were as dear to his heart as Aphrodite.

There are many stories that include Hephaestus's inventions. One included his creation of a man. Hephaestus, Athena, and Poseidon were arguing over who was the best craftsman. Momus was asked to judge a contest of skill among the gods. Momus was the god of ridicule and scorn. The gods would later regret choosing him. Each of the three gods presented what they thought was their best invention. Hephaestus created a man. Athena built a house. Poseidon made a bull. Momus was always quick to criticize. So he immediately pointed out the flaws in each god's creation.

He said that Poseidon's bull should have eyes under its horns. This would allow the bull to aim at what it was trying to stab with its horns. To Athena, he complained that her house did not have wheels. How else would its owners take it with them when they traveled? Momus finally reached Hephaestus's invention. He wanted to know why they had not put a window in the chest of the man. A window would allow his neighbors to see what he was planning. Zeus was furious and forever banned Momus from Mount Olympus.

Zeus was angry with the men on Earth. The Titan Prometheus had convinced them to trick Zeus. So Zeus came up with a plan to punish them all. Zeus asked Hephaestus to create a beautiful maiden. Hephaestus made her from clay, and the gods gave her many gifts. Aphrodite gave her beauty, Hermes gave her persuasion, and Apollo gave her music. She was named Pandora, which means "all-gifted." When she was complete, the goddess Athena clothed Pandora and breathed life into her. Zeus gave her some gifts as well. He gave Pandora a deep curiosity. Zeus also gave Pandora a sealed box. He told her she was never to open it.

Zeus then sent Pandora to Earth to marry a human. She was happy, but she could never forget the sealed box. One day she could not resist the temptation any longer. Pandora decided to take just one peek. What could it hurt? When Pandora opened the box, all the evils of the world escaped. Unknown to man, these curses would torment all humans. Things such as greed, vanity, and jealousy affected how people felt. Pandora managed to close the box right before hope had escaped, too. Zeus had placed hope at the bottom of the box. As long as there was hope, all was not lost. Zeus had succeeded in getting his revenge.

Smart, skilled and generous, Hephaestus had only one downfall—his appearance. Hephaestus had earned the respect of the other gods. They loved his inventions and fabulous gifts. Yet he was never really an equal because he was ugly and lame.

Metalworkers and blacksmiths worshipped Hephaestus. His temples were located all over Greece in the manufacturing and industrial centers. Hephaestus had several feasts and festivals held in his honor. During the Chalceia festival in Athens, his worshippers came together to celebrate his invention of bronze working.

The Roman god Vulcan was similar to Hephaestus. Vulcan was also the god of fire. However, Vulcan was associated with the damaging side of fire. His worshippers prayed to him to prevent fires. Vulcan began to take on the qualities of Hephaestus when Rome invaded Greece. Hephaestus may have had a minor role in the Greek myths, but the god of fire was important to the blacksmiths, craftsmen, and metalworkers of the ancient world.

TEMPLE OF HEPHAESTUS

In 449 BC, a beautiful temple was begun overlooking the Agora in Athens. The Agora was the marketplace and civic center. It was one of the most important parts of the ancient city. It was built to honor Hephaestus. The temple's dominant position in the city shows how important Hephaestus was as the god of craftsmen. The Temple of Hephaestus is a beautifully preserved example of ancient Greek architecture.

PRINCIPAL GODS OF GREEK MYTHOLOGY
A FAMILY TREE

THE ROMAN GODS

As the Roman Empire expanded by conquering new lands, the Romans often took on aspects of the customs and beliefs of the people they conquered. From the ancient Greeks they took their arts and sciences. They also adopted many of their gods and the myths that went with them into their religious beliefs. While the names were changed, the stories and legends found a new home.

ZEUS: Jupiter
King of the Gods, God of Sky and Storms
Symbols: Eagle and Thunderbolt

HERA: Juno
Queen of the Gods, Goddess of Marriage
Symbols: Peacock, Cow, and Crow

POSEIDON: Neptune
God of the Sea and Earthquakes
Symbols: Trident, Horse, and Dolphin

HADES: Pluto
God of the Underworld
Symbols: Helmet, Metals, and Jewels

ATHENA: Minerva
Goddess of Wisdom, War, and Crafts
Symbols: Owl, Shield, and Olive Branch

ARES: Mars
God of War
Symbols: Vulture and Dog

ARTEMIS: Diana
Goddess of Hunting and Protector of Animals
Symbols: Stag and Moon

APOLLO: Apollo
God of the Sun, Healing, Music, and Poetry
Symbols: Laurel, Lyre, Bow, and Raven

HEPHAESTUS: Vulcan
God of Fire, Metalwork, and Building
Symbols: Fire, Hammer, and Donkey

APHRODITE: Venus
Goddess of Love and Beauty
Symbols: Dove, Sparrow, Swan, and Myrtle

EROS: Cupid
God of Love
Symbols: Quiver and Arrows

HERMES: Mercury
God of Travels and Trade
Symbols: Staff, Winged Sandals, and Helmet

FURTHER INFORMATION

BOOKS

Green, Jen. *Ancient Greek Myths*. New York: Gareth Stevens, 2010.

Napoli, Donna Jo. *Treasury of Greek Mythology: Classic Stories of Gods, Goddesses, Heroes & Monsters*. Washington, DC: National Geographic Society, 2011.

Reusser, Kayleen. *Hephaestus*. Hockessin, DE: Mitchell Lane Publishers, 2010.

WEBSITES

Visit our website for links about Hephaestus: **childsworld.com/links**

Note to Parents, Teachers, and Librarians: We routinely verify our Web links to make sure they are safe and active sites. So encourage your readers to check them out!

INDEX